ALL ART IS JUNK

R. A. HARRIS

Bizarro Pulp Press
www.BIZARROPULPPRESS.com
All Art is Junk Copyright © 2013 R. A. Harris
Matthew Revert Copyright © 2013
 www.matthewrevert.com - Cover Design

ISBN-13: 978-0615791791

ISBN-10: 0615791794

Printed in the USA.

Author's Acknowledgements

I would like to thank Pat Douglas at Bizarro Pulp Press for giving me a shot at the big time. I would also like to thank you, the reader, for giving me the opportunity to entertain you. May your life be charmed.

Chapter 1

The dry heaving pipes of the dead jet pack sucking cold air sound like a low blood sugar level orchestra playing a piss poor staccato symphony, a hive of electronic farts played in super-slowmo. I press the ignition button repeatedly, the spark a strobing star, but there's no fuel for it to catch and ignite. The sun grins over the horizon behind us. We begin to descend, a sentient cymbal crescendo swan diving towards the final note of a fractured cadence. Scanning for a viable landing zone confirms presupposition. We aren't supposed to survive this one. This is the end of the tour.

Beneath us is a square mile island, most of it coated in a cruel blaze, mockingly eating the fuel we desperately need to keep us aloft. Beyond the flames the ocean beats the coast senseless from all sides, jagged waves curling over sagging rock dragging yet more land to the merciless deep. Men, foolish enough to venture that they were sailors, slap like landed fish against the rubble of their ships piled in Gimp Cove, the current pinning the vestiges to the edge of the land.

A thick shadow, thicker than even the heaviest rain cloud could muster, covers us as a teetering salmon flesh pink tower curls over us from behind. A giant finger rising from the ground come to squash us like a pest. Only this finger is made of hundreds of human bodies stacked like Jenga blocks, all elbows and knees and teeth grinding and flaking. As it leans in towards us, I sense her. She's there in the stack, almost anonymous amongst the mess of limbs and torsos jerking and swimming in the air trying to right the massive pink pillar, save it from face planting into the flaming ground. I thought our connection would have died by now but I recognize her trace signature. It's in my code. The tower swings back the other way, unveiling the morning sun, white light expanding like a ray gun blast. I turn and watch as the column sways back and forth like a comedic waiter carrying a tray of dishes containing jelly. Super zoom in to see her squawking face, cheeks stretched white like stressed plastic. Packed into the human skyscraper, a victim crushed in a gangbang orgy.

I've found Lana at last. She's become one of the totems. As we slowly cascade down towards the burning ground I throw the spare life ring I held onto towards her. It falls short as the flesh tower block bends away from us. Some opportunists further down the pile grab hold instead, anchoring us to the towering populace. We swing like Tarzan and Jane towards it. The screams of our landing zone are cut short by my steel feet smashing through pathetic skull bones like bricks through windows. I grasp onto spare limbs, using all my strength, causing the brittle bones to crumble like shortcrust pastry in my grip, strawberry sauce squirting out. We swing in a fancy arc away from the broken bodies, a lead pendulum balloon. The anchor slips and arms pulled from sockets come hurtling towards us as blood rains down, painting us ruby red. I sever the last of my laserwire to release the ring, and it spins away like an Olympic discus.

"What the fuck is going on?" Cilia has woken up. Her usual chipper self replaced by the semi-conscious demon princess strapped to my back, shocked back to life by a defibrillator in the form of freshly amputated limbs slapping her in the face.

"We are rapidly descending towards the Earth," I tell her, "and the ground is on fire."

"Then fucking deploy the crash landing gear according to protocol," she rips. A mechanical distorted oscillation tells me she has returned to snoozing immediately.

She is logical almost to a fault. I deploy the crash landing gear according to protocol without resistance: I press the CLP switch, ejecting the empty jet pack from my back and releasing seven thousand liters of compressed whipped cream from the emergency canister, it coats the Earth like a bukkake scene. The swarming fire melts most of it by the time we smack into the ground. The remaining cream doesn't slow our velocity even one iota and the soft ground swallows us like we're a bullet fired down a well.

Cilia remains rock-like in her sleep. The morning sky peeks in through the entrance to our cavity, a perfect Junk and Cilia shape some two hundred meters above, an angel bird in flight made of sleepy orange steadily blushing blue. Rain drops decanter onto Cilia's sensor, deforming the world.

The ground shakes violently as a thousand drums steam roll art on top of us, burying us deep and dirty in the bowels of The Installation.

Chapter 2

The drum had been a constant since the deluge. A wild discordant beast, atemporal and offbeat. A chainsaw revolving at 0.01 rpm or there abouts, decay reverberating like a gunshot on the moors. The moment after Lana disappeared it became my death knell, signifying my grave was being dug in soft ground. A keeper without his quarry was as useful as a chocolate fireguard. A redundancy of metal and flesh, true to my name.

I was ingested by a jungle of people that grew about me as they spilled from the only nightclub on the island, their breath and cognition fermented. I began asking in earnest if they had seen Lana: she had somehow slipped the noose. Jaundiced faces lit by flickering torch and sinewy moonlight, escorted on bow legs and twisting feet, blankly gazed into my sensor as if looking at a rock or modern art installation. That drum spasm lashing like a whip occasioned a punctuation mark on my inquiry. Within moments the crowd had dispersed and I was left alone, regurgitated and holding the laserwire that should have been connecting me to Lana limply in my rusted hands. The last fifteen years of successfully fulfilling my sole task had effectively been negated in a single moment. A discontinuity, a blip, a segment of ruin deleting the previous data storage one and a half decades long, enough to fill ten landfill sites over.

Then, a colossal clang that set my clocks back to zero and violently shook connectors out of their ports ripped through the air. I immediately set my EM scanner to infrared, looking for the trademark balloon of white heat outlined in the tangerine orange of an explosion, but there was nothing amiss: the surrounding area was as cold as ever, a quiet purple hue, steady and calm, the wavering orange warmth of the crowd dissipating—leaving me, a lonely cloud. Soon, the only heat was in my head, like I'd been baptized in fire. It was a shameful heat, red blooded and clammy, melting my circuits, confusing and overloading my primary processors. I blew out smoke rings, red hot copper wire vaporized in my cheeks. I immediately blamed the laserwire. Antiquated technology from before The Installation.

I remember bringing the error in choosing such a connecting tissue up with Jessica, Lana's deceased mother. "Physical connections are ancient. Technology lets us communicate to each other through immaterial waves now, Jessica," I told her.

"If you can't feel each other how can you tell when you aren't in contact any more, Lancelot?" She implored me with glinting eyes, the same her daughter used on me in times of disagreement. The kind I wish Cilia would use, rather than her hacksaw tongue and razor wit. "I would feel so much more secure knowing she was bound to you by your strong grip. Besides, the laserwires today are supposed to be stronger than spiderweb a meter thick."

She had stumped me. I couldn't be sure how

I would know we were still in contact without that physical tension between us. I might be receiving ghost messages, merely phantom exchanges created by a subconscious part of my server and looped back to me via a hidden circuit. It wasn't my place to second-guess my mistress either. After all, she was the human. I acquiesced and held tightly onto the laserwire, immediately falling in love with the calming series of baby-innocent thoughts pulsing brightly like a new born star.

Retracing my steps seemed the logical things to do. I must have waylaid her inside the club. I figured she was still at the bar, waiting for her ward to return. There's no way Mansell would have gotten to her already.

Chapter 3

Lana sat up on my shoulders until she was too big to fit. Or too big to want to fit. I could have lifted her a hundred times over, even as a full grown adult.

"You have the name of a knight, Lancelot. And yet you have been my steed for too long now," she said as she climbed down for the last time. The weight of her maturity lifting off me was far greater than her petite mass. "Rise, sir Lancelot," she said, a giggling princess.

I rose from my knee, my chest a mighty shield, embossed and shining with the pride of the sun.

Lana took to skipping in front of me, her steady rhythm coalescing with the pulses of my circulatory system, all chattering beeps and slanting whirs. The paintbrushes in her hair splattering the path before us with a myriad of beautiful colours.

There was no logic to it, just the coalescence of colours into unrecognizable patterns, but somehow smoldering with intent and inherent meaning.

Chapter 4

Two sensor devices stood on corroded iron bars guarding the entrance, their senile faces covered in dust. They had never worked. I stepped past them and into the club.

The floor was sticky with spilled fluid. Nasty toxic light meant it was easier for me to see in ultraviolet, so I switched my sensor over. Purple dissonance led me across a dance floor populated by disintegrated prophylactics and needles still oozing oil. It was easier to ignore it when I had Lana to watch over. So long as she wasn't harmed, the others could pump themselves full of metamorphosed plants and animals until they grew fur for all I cared. They say it unleashes their inner beast. My inner beast is a quantum processor. I think I'd just start finding roots of imaginary numbers if I ever 'shot the sap'. It was times like these I wish Lana and I were connected via the waves.

Lana wasn't anywhere to be found. Not a scent, not a whisper of her. Just the hounding lights and immolated plants reincarnated as a drug and deified as life changing escapism. I turned to leave, unsure as to where Lana could have been, when I stepped on a familiar object. It was one of Lana's paintbrush hairs. A quick analysis revealed it was stained with blood. Her blood. The worst possible scenarios trampled through my brain, shutting auxiliary processes down. I could only replay one thought: Mansell had taken her, had killed her. I had absolutely failed. I would have committed *harakiri* at that moment, but it wouldn't have done any good. Chips for organs.

I slammed a fist into the wall beside me, striking an electrical box on the side. The schizophrenic lights died and were replaced by ancient humming tubes kicking out yellow sodium light. I stood transfixed by the pattern on the floor. Lana's paint had miraculously formed a sentient image of a cyborg with two heads and a sour man driving it onwards. Mansell. I really was too late.

I left the club, kicking the dusty simulacra of security over as I passed them by.

Chapter 5

Lana screamed as she attempted to slam the bedroom door; the laserwire flashed brilliantly as it defied the steel force, sending the door back out in a wide arc. Her eyes, glassy electric hawks, bore into me from her sanctuary, open like a book, pop-up images swimming along the laserwire.

"Your mother was not evil and I am not retarded, Lana," I said.

"Then let me the fuck out of my room!"

"You know I can't. Your mother was very specific about that. It's just not safe for you out there," I repeated the scripture from my core as I stepped into the blank canvas room, shutting the steel door behind me.

"You've told me shit! Why would he want to kill me? It doesn't make sense! I'm his daughter for fuck sake!" Lana threw herself onto her mattress, seismic waves convulsing her body. Her pillow rainbow stained.

I stood still. A dumb statue, a surrogate parent image without the correct protocol.

" Lana, it's me: Lancelot, your shield, your knight," was all I could think to say.

"You aren't a knight, you're just junk!"

Chapter 6

Others would always tell me I should do more to appreciate art. The subtle nuances it gives to a voice disharmonious to your own can help craft entirely new fabrics of reality to clothe yourself in. "Wash your world in the colours of another's vision," they'd say. "Enhance the scripture you use to justify your beliefs through others' interpretation of the world. Breathe new aromas, breed new thoughts, feel new emotions."

I knew that the only art I ever cared for was Lana's, and that was just an offshoot of her essence, not a conscious apprehension of conceit like those others, the ones who did it for the money, or even for love. There was no love in Lana's art, only an imminent sense of being.

I decided that art was as much about the destitution of the materials and colours used in its inception as it was about the production of "new, visceral experiences and concepts". I concluded it was more about aesthetic than utility, power over material and over others' minds, subversive as opposed to constructive. The Installation proved me wrong.

The largest piece of art ever commissioned. An island off the south-west coast of England, made of the relics of an ancient time regurgitated in modern timbre, a time of little consequence and uncapped growth. It was to plant the seeds of ideas unfathomable in the current cultural milieu of the world. The entire planet had become unidirectional. All signs pointed west. The island bore no such signature. No artist claimed responsibility for it. It had that quality about it I recognized in Lana's art. It was art made of being and nothing more. It was simply known as The Tnstallation and without it, terrestrial life would have become extinct.

Twenty years ago, the waters escalated. Plastic tides bearing the grinning corpses of fish and whales brought cities to their knees. Entire continents were submerged by an oceanic deluge.

Only The Installation remained. An aesthetic

comment turned utile ark. A subversion turned savior, much to my intrigue and puzzlement.

Plastic trees and tin cans turned forest and city, rusted cars and farm machinery turned home and hospital. Diverse wildlife turned domestic pets, humanity turned humdrum populace of so many Caucasians. Life became monochromatic and wretched, modern art all.

Chapter 7

Outside the club I wandered onto a street lit by lanterns overhead. A lone woman strolled along the length of the street, jabbering to herself. I caught what she was saying as she passed by.

"There's a Turkish delight, a cat whose gums are slack. There's a Turkish delight, a cat whose gums are slack. There's a Turkish delight, a cat whose gums are slack." The lady's gums smacked together as she repeated her mantra, spittle trails hung like spiderweb between them. She was walking her cat on a laserwire, a little black ball of muddied, stiff fur that nervously led her down the street and back again, tentatively sniffing at me before skipping away in a heartbeat.

I sat on the curb edge, beside a gutter full of yesteryear's newspapers, clogging up the infrastructure. Wall Street collapses, terrorist attacks, Olympic ceremony, an occult festival summoning forth a sea demon far grander than the rotten cultists fathomed. Nostalgia is not something I feel innately, but I understand it to be something similar to what I feel when I think about how it used to be with Lana. It feels like a program was uninstalled from my system but the user didn't delete the desktop shortcut and another user is trying to run the program by clicking the icon. Some data still exists that reminds me there was a program I used to run. I was suddenly struck by the notion that the lady with the cat was probably suffering from nostalgia. A ringing snare drum shot, louder than ever before, powered around us, toppling the street lanterns over. Their fires neatly extinguished in the puddles collected in the streets like lost lagoons, gentle hisses like decaying sighs. The lady didn't notice. Perhaps she was deaf. She was in another world. Rain started to sprinkle us, her wrinkled skin repelling the beads of water running down her bald head. The paint covering me ran down into the street, leaving my pale metal skin bared against the water. The rust in my joints sang praise to the weather king, squeaking a cacophony as I stood. Lana was long gone. Probably executed already.

I would find Cilia; her logical circuit was more complex than mine and she could see further than I could. She'd know what to do if Lana had been executed. Perhaps just shut me down. Recycle me so I would be useful again.

Chapter 8

A slender arm, no wider than the bone entombed in the pale flesh about it, twists and comes apart at the joints. Bone and cartilage scrape together as ligaments and tendons tear away from their anchor points. The gurgled scream accompanying the destruction of the limb is cut short by a steel toe cap disintegrating jaw, teeth and cheek. A slack maw slippery with lifeless tongue and pink frothy spit kisses the earth before it, tastes defeat. Red-stained dirt clings to the torn fabric of the face as it's raised on a strength swelling from somewhere beyond reason, beyond pain; pride, coughing strings of bloodied snot, emanating from teary eyes props it, endears it. Eyes surrounded by molten bone swirling behind storm-cloud-bruised cheeks. Not a word, but a look. A million looks to give and this one that cuts the worst. This one that incenses the worst. Something dark, something putrid, something calling out to a force inhuman. A pitifully human voice augments the sensation. "I love you," It says. The phonemes clatter over loose teeth and cascade down trembling tongue.

In response: a controlled nod, calculated, sombre. Then a surging energy separates the head from torso, voice from mouth. A fountain of carotid blood jettisons across the floorboards, coal dark and thick like cooled lava.

"This is what love looks like. The violence of love is the most beautiful thing," says a voice, breath of steaming air, saturated with crystallized knives forged in the fiery pit of damned love. "This is what love feels like," it continues, grey fingers curling through the red soup, letting it sift through them, splashing into the pool spreading across the dirty ground. The palm of the hand smears blood across the floor into a rudimentary shape, a family and its home.

Mansell Rivers pats the two heads of his cyborg, anointing them with the blood of his deceased wife, Jessica. "You did good, little ones. We'll try something different tomorrow." His feet are dark with congealed blood, his face a mask of quiet deliverance.

Chapter 9

I left the old lady walking her cat to her own devices, making my way through the market district. The shops weren't really shops, more just stacks of objects that had a similar aesthetic effect on people. There were many arguments over which objects should go in which pile, how to divide them: was it shape, size, color, or use that affected people the most? Hence the bartering system: a series of thefts and gifts, the replacement of objects taken by something deemed more suitable to the location.

Though it was always in a state of flux, the market achieved the rudimentary function of allowing people to trade without always having to resort to violence. Those who spent their time picking through the piles were adamant this was the natural state of the market. There was some larger force at work, organizing things.

When violence was needed, it was always

arbitrated and conducted by Mansell Rivers. Of course, his two headed cyborg behemoth allowed him to control the people; everybody knew it, but knowing and acting are not the same thing. It was the two-headed cyborg that Lana's paintbrush hair had managed to paint in the club.

There seemed to be more activity than normal; on each beat of the mighty electronic snare new people would turn up and begin sorting the piles. For once, they were working in tandem. A production line formed which sorted the foods from the non-foods. The carbs from the non-carbs. The sugars from the non-sugars.

I realized I didn't have time to stand around and watch them, even though it was a sentimental and heartwarming occurrence to see them slowly rebuilding a society shaken to within an inch of its life. As I left the market zone, more people were streaming in. They all had sugar glazed expressions on their faces, jerked into animated laughter only by the thundering drum, which became more omnipresent with each stroke. The striking, evil drum thundering into my core.

Chapter 10

"God, I hate you so much!"

"You're a fucking crybaby!"

"Gross, loser."

People have always telepathically abused him. It's the main reason he has become a stay at home dad. Avoiding any and all social interactions as best he can. It doesn't save him from his children's scorn though. Nor that of his wife. Their constant derision has been enough to turn his genius evil. And if there is one thing the world doesn't need after being royally fucked by a flood of biblical proportions, it's an evil genius.

Three of his children caw and wail at him as his most heinous invention yet slides its rusty scissor claws around their frail necks. They clap shut, decapitating all three in one snip.

"That's a father's love for you," he says to himself, telepathically. His is the only voice that truly understands him and his art. "I know it is," he replies, a tear rolling over his lip, breaching his mouth. The saltiness is abhorrent.

He dips a brush into the nearest child's chest cavity, right down through the bronchii, so the bristles splinter into the alveoli. The mucus mixed with blood makes an excellent base coat. He wipes the fluid across his face. He is the canvass, the artist and the audience. The only one who truly understands his art.

His two-headed cyborg transforms into a chariot and he steps onto its back. They ride away from the killing room, the wheels leaving a trail of blood like arms out stretching for a hug.

Chapter 11

I reached Lana's room while it was still dark. The paintings on her wall had an ethereal sentiment at that late hour. I could imagine Lana drifting to sleep, dreaming of their indigo voices singing harmonies to her. I didn't know what they were of; a teenage girl has secrets that even a laserwire cannot transmit, but I felt they were honest and beautiful. I added it to my criteria of what art is; real art is, the art of *being*. I quickly scavenged the room for the key to unlock Cilia. I found it beneath Lana's diary, which I still did not dare look inside, if only because she may yet be alive and I couldn't bear for her to connect with me through the laserwire and know I had read it.

I pulled my chest plate down and placed the key in the drive. A humming surge of electric current from Cilia's starter motor passed through me, before giving way to the powerful kicks as her engine revved into life. Cilia's cranky limbs extended from my back, along with a scraping voice asking what time it was.

"Check your internal clock," I said, throwing my arms up.

"I broke it, damn thing kept telling me to wake up." I felt Cilia shift right, and then left. "Where's Lana?" she asked, over my shoulder.

"Lana Rivers is missing."

After a moment, "Did you check last known location?"

"Yes. She wasn't there."

"Did you ask locals for information?"

"Yes. They didn't see her."

"Did you alert me?"

"Yes. Just now."

"Then we are to approach Mansell Rivers at this time, where we shall either kick him in the face, crush his organs and retrieve Lana, or we shall kick him in the face, crush his organs and fail to retrieve Lana."

"Understood," I said.

A rhythmic series of oscillations indicated

Cilia was asleep again. I set out towards Mansell Rivers' house.

Chapter 12

A light rain still fell outside. My joints creaked and snarled as I walked across the boggy ground. It was mostly made of toilet tissue and old egg cartons. Jessica and I decided it was best to keep Lana's profile as low as possible, out of the way of the other people. Nobody came out this way; this part of The Installation wasn't aesthetically pleasing and didn't serve any utile purpose, aside from our need for a secluded area, of course. It was surprising to see a motley crowd of about twenty or so people spread around us in a circle. They all wore armor made of incongruous metal pieces. Each was a genderless structure of misappropriated material. They looked like Transformers if the Transformers had been scrapped and left to rust for twenty years, or extras from Mad Max that didn't get the memo that shooting had finished. Car doors were held as shields, axles and drive shafts with flaming tires on the top stood erect from their backs, steering wheels with nefarious spikes attached to them spun on the end of chains. Radiators had been corrupted into what looked like missile launchers, refrigerator piping converted into freeze guns, souls screeched in metal cacophony. LEDs and dials flashed across computer monitors attached as visors and artificial light glazed on their screens. I switched to infrared; a soft orange glow burned inside each suit.

"We saw you coming in here, cyborg. No use in hiding," the one nearest us said. Their voice contorted by a mask made of metal torn from any number of contraptions—a junk yard on their face.

"I'm not hiding, I'm right here," I said, confused.

"We'll tear your guts out!" One of them shouted as if incensed by what I said.

Another came out with, "We'll use your skull box as a shoe!"

The one who had spoken first stepped forward and said coyly, "We just want your flesh is all, fella."

"I am made of metal, my flesh is not accessible without engineering tools." Even as I said it I knew they probably had the gear for the job, or at least, had fashioned something capable of performing the rudiments of the task, if not with surgical precision.

"Then we'll just take your skin." Sudden anger boiled in their voice, modulating it even further from human to machine. They rushed me. For armor they wore a great turquoise car bonnet chest plate dulled by a ubiquitous layer of grease and streaked with maroon rust. On their shoulders they had two alloy pads, both had spikes protruding from them at dangerous angles. Their fists were covered in oil, which they set alight by scraping them across their thighs like matches as they came nearer. Their pupils reflected the orange glow of their fists like two distant stars as they leapt at me. I side-stepped the shooting star and slammed a fist down onto their head, caving it in like a metal Pavlova. The others didn't appreciate that and all charged us at the same time.

"I apologize for murdering that person," I tried to tell them, but the sound of igniting engines drowned out my voice. And then the drum struck again, faster than before, followed by a second distinct smack. There were two drums playing now. The crowd of metal meat-heads came at us, oil and blood and metal and flesh scraping and bumping and sliding together.

I ran to meet them, bringing my hand over my eyes so I didn't have to see what carnage I was about to cause. I felt metal crumple like sheets of paper beneath my feet, bones turn to dust and blood vessels burst from the sudden intense pressure of having a ton of metal pressed onto chests or necks or heads. I didn't stop running, even when I felt the ground soften and the sounds of the engines die out; I didn't stop running even as I ran over a cliff edge. The drums had picked up the pace, almost matching my pulsing electronics in their intensity and speed and that was all I heard as I fell.

Chapter 13

Mansell Rivers is still unsatisfied with the feeling of power it gives him to snuff the members of his family. It's because of Lana. The daughter who got away. He just needs to get near her for a short while, to extract some DNA (and then murder her in cold blood), and everything will be settled and he will be able to happily relinquish control of the island, and with it, all of the remaining life on the planet, well *almost* all of the remaining life on the planet. Her constant telepathic abuse from some unknown location is a source of immense embarrassment and shame on the part of Mansell. How can he claim to be an evil genius when he can't even destroy his weak daughter? He has the tools— he crafted them himself. Far superior to his wife's pathetic attempt at creating artificial life.

***

"There is no way a cyborg can fall in love. Listen to yourself, Jess!" He had said.

"I don't care what you say, Mansell, I am building these two together. Two heads are better than one."

She had been right about that last part, Mansell conceded. But two monstrous heads are far better than two humanoid heads. That's why his cyborg has two tyrannosaur skulls and can fire lasers from its eyes.

"The tenderness of a stroke is something that even a cyborg should know how to apply," Jessica had said as she stroked his balding head one night, near the end.

He disagreed with that. Physical connection is just a way for people to enforce their psychic torment on him. That's why his cyborg has the power to crush steel and diamond, and human bodies of course. It pops them like a bag of sweets, entrails exploding like the innards of a pick'n'mix. Their brains flop onto the ground before being swallowed by his cyborg. Yes, his cyborg runs on human brains. It was part of his evil genius to devise a cyborg that does that. If he could just devour every brain in existence he would be free of the torment and ridicule wrought upon him by the soft pink balls of mush, thinking themselves safe in their bone castles.

Chapter 14

A side effect of the market becoming absolutely free has been the redundancy of shopping lists. No longer needed, thousands and thousands of them were tossed out to sea only to be returned to The Installation by the unrelenting tide, as if to say none shall escape. Sometimes it seems like the island isn't so much a savior as a prison. The lists were swept up along the coast towards 'The Gullet', a slender cove with an overhang affectionately dubbed 'The Chubby Uvula'. From there they were brought inland along muddy channels of water, permanent brown streaks that flowed against the ebb of the tide before being dumped in a waterhole, the water stodgy with paper mushed together after many years of collecting.

Surrounding the waterhole were a number of seasons of the high street fashion clothes still on the rails. They had been brought along by the truckload even before the flood destroyed 99.99% of the planet. Nobody liked fashion; everybody wanted to wear their own iconoclastic garbs. Most fashionistas had tried donning that particular niche, shriveling it quicker than a slug in salt. Now the clothes that sported killer phrases and satirical images of pop culture hung like bodies on a gallows, gently swaying in the twilight wind. Most people got by completely naked, though some still retained a pre-apocalyptic sense of shame brought about by Christian texts (revered with a renewed interest immediately following the deluge, but soon discarded in favor of more intense, intravenous fetishes) and covered their genitalia with customized milk cartons or mugs suctioned on with water.

I knew our best bet of avoiding the gang of metal fetishists would be a disguise, so I unwrapped a few different clothes and threw them over us. Although we were clothed head to toe in fashionable items, we looked outstandingly bad. A military style jacket with the words 'guns ain't got shit on my dick!' scrawled across the back in white paint over a couple of t-shirts—each endowed with a heap of opposite images to represent the notion of a binary reality, a fascist attempt at coercing people into accepting one way of living by creating a false dilemma, a disjunctive either/or statement with no real equivalence, but of course, people lapped such overt fascist concepts up before the apocalypse, and after too. I stepped into some loose fitting lounge pants, as no other style would fit. They tore as I dragged them over my legs, so my bottom half looked like an early twenty-first century pirate who spent his time in his comfortable home on a comfortable sofa but still donned the style of his peers. Unless I was very much mistaken, the guise would hold.

"Cilia, which way is it to Mansell Rivers' home?"

An electronic buzz like a piston made of fire. "Due East, two clicks."

"Good, we should make it there before sunrise."

"Negative, radar shows incoming hostiles,

numbering some thirty in number."

"The machine people?"

"Too early to say. Best we mingle, see if we can't make use of your cunning disguise." If I were a betting cyborg, I would have laid a heap of coins down that she was being impudent.

I casually strutted about the area, looking over clothes that would never be worn, trying my best to look like a consumer. There were hoods with caps in them and water proof pants with holes in them and t-shirts with no neck hole and a slash in the belly to look out of and suits made of spandex and shoes that counted how many times you swore and rewarded you with sweets and loads more, each more stupid and inane than the last.

Soon enough, a small herd of people came over a brow from the East, chasing after the old woman with the cat on a leash. Her bald head was visibly respiring, sweat curling away from it like interstellar dust from a comet.

"Why would they be chasing such a sweet looking lady?" I pondered to myself. Then I saw it.

Their hands. A variety of domestic animals had been weaponized by inserting fists into their anuses. Dogs snarled with anal-invasive rage, cats hissed and flicked claws like daggers as their sphincters were violated, lizards blew their cheeks and throats up, opening jaws wider than ever before as thumbs and fingers compacted into their rectums. I realized their intentions with a sickening feeling. Not helped by the whirlwind of drums that had begun to pick up pace and intensity.

"There's a Turkish delight, a cat whose gums are slack!" The old lady bellowed, nearly out of breath as she was.

"Do we help her?" I asked Cilia.

"Negative, we are to kick Mansell Rivers until he is dead."

I don't understand what it was that made me want to help the lady. Maybe because I had met her before and decided that she was suffering enough; to see her now in such a state made my processor short-circuit. Maybe I was just one of the good ones. I quickly stepped into the path of the oncoming traffic.

"There's a Turkish delight..." the woman cried as she ran past me.

A moment later the rabble engulfed us. A woman with a fish on each finger squeezed through the crowd on top of us and slapped my face. Cat claws tore through the loose fabric, squealing on the metal beneath. Dog jaws wrapped around my wrists and parrots pecked at my sensor, cracking the screen, oil colours spilled into each other. I fell backwards in a flurry. Cilia wailed beneath me that she was injured and I was a fool. This was why Lana was missing. Jessica was a fool to trust me for any longer than twelve years with the care of her child. I broke a dog's neck, wringing it clean of blood.

"Shut up Cilia, I'm trying to get us out of this!"

"Start defense line alpha protocol," she replied, her patience dried up.

"I can't see."

"Then I'll patch you in my feed."

I stared into a discarded shopping list, so close I could see its fibers. The very core of its being was open to me. The intricate lacing of thread through a delicate fabric dyed with an ink made of a thousand different bugs and plants, not industrially mixed, either. This was no ordinary shopping list. Somebody took the time to painstakingly create this list from rare materials. The words didn't immediately strike me as meaningful, but that is not to say that this list couldn't be the exact recipe for mine and Cilia's, and Lana's, survival. However, it was useless where it was.

"Pick that paper up," I said to Cilia.

"What paper?"

"The piece I'm looking at."

"We're being eaten by pets and you want me to pick up a piece of paper? What happened to defense line alpha protocol?"

"I'll do it after you grab that list. I think it might be important." I hoped it was. Incurring Cilia's wrath was never something to be taken lightly. She made a clunk noise like maybe she was pissed off, but picked up the list anyway.

"Activating defense line alpha protocol now."

"Remember to set it 180 degrees."

"Yes, of course!" I snapped, aware that it was lucky she had reminded me. I rotated the defense line 180 degrees and fired it up. Liquid death exploded from every pour on our body, melting the faces of the animals unlucky enough to be chomping down on us at that moment. The liquid death didn't stop there; it climbed along the body of the animals, dissolving the sick puppeteers arms and then their torsos, before finally engulfing their heads, brains boiling in their skulls before evaporating through their eye sockets and nasal cavities.

We stood and ran backwards. In a matter of bounds we had caught up to the little lady, her cat was bouncing along behind her, neck nearly broken from being tugged so hard.

"—Gums that are slack!" I heard her finish saying as we approached.

"Pick her up."

Cilia didn't like being told what to do. "It is neither logical, nor in our interest to save this woman."

"I already lost one person tonight and I'm not about to lose another. Pick her up!"

Cilia swore in mechanical jargon, all acid corrosive. I hoped the little old lady couldn't understand it, as some of it was aimed at her.

"I don't know what's gotten into you, Junk," she continued, "You've gone off the matrix."

"The matrix wasn't made to deal with grief."

"Grief?"

"I miss Lana. I need her back and I am acting irrationally based on some emotional data not accounted for in the initial calculations by Jessica."

"Don't you try to blame Jessica, fool though she was for creating you when I would suffice."

"There's a Turkish deli—"

Cilia scooped the woman up and threw her over our shoulders. She smelled of spices. The cat dangled, swinging like a pendulum.

"I'm taking over my sight again." Everything went black for a moment before a dizzying display of technicolor spread before me. It was like Lana was there, shaking her wild hair in my face again.

"I'm taking the woman to the shopping district. There's a lot of commotion over there. She should be a discrete addition. After that I need a rest. I will give you control of my limbs. You are to take us straight to Mansell Rivers' house."

"Understood." Lana's locks fell away from my face and I was left looking at colors without emotion, bleak light mixed with disinterest as Cilia bore me and the woman on her back.

Chapter 15

Lana was different to the other children. Her hair for one. Always swishing about, creating masterpieces of art that would easily have rivaled the biggest names in history, and always done with such innocence, such truth. The other two twins were your average children. Their art was mediocre, terrible even. They neither excelled nor lagged at anything, they simply ambled along, almost like background. There was something else though, about Lana, something that came across as almost unreal because it was so genuine. She was a princess, in an ontic sense. Jessica knew she had to build her a knight, but a knight worthy of such an acute royalty. Royalty not in any sense of power or control, but royalty in her love and compassion for life and being. It shone in her art, timeless beauty sung from behind the shapes and colors that fell from Lana's hair. Yes, it had to be a knight capable of love.

"That's why I am giving you Lancelot," she had said to Lana one evening.

"Oh wow, really?" Her eyes lighting up with charitable excitement.

Lancelot shone like a star next to Jessica, smiling sheepishly.

"And Cilia, of course," Jessica added, feeling good about the warmth her child showed the cyborgs. Cilia flashed a red LED and clicked some strange noises.

"Cilia is rude!"

"That's rude!"

Lana blushed.

"I'll tell her to be nice to you," Jessica said, smiling at her child's humility.

Lana smiled too, but then the smile died as she thought of something. "Why don't you tell Daddy to be nice?"

Jessica felt like she'd been slapped. She managed to recover herself and said, "Your daddy isn't like Cilia—he won't listen to me."

"But you're so strong, everybody listens to

you."

"Even strong women like me can't get through to everybody, Lana. Your daddy shut the world out long ago. The most we can do is avoid him."

"But you go to him every night. I see you."

"What?"

"Every night you return to him. Every day you are reborn. I saw it happen."

Jessica looked at her daughter in horror, her mouth flapping. She grabbed her and pulled her head in, hugging it tightly to her chest. "You must never go near him, Lana, swear to me you won't."

"I swear, Jessica."

"Good girl. You're such a bright girl. I know I can trust you. Lancelot will be good to you."

"I love you, Jessica."

"I love you too." Jessica's eyes said it was the truth, but it was a painful, regrettable truth.

Chapter 16

Cilia strode in time to the drums as we ran across the refuse landscape. I counted eighteen different ones now, cycling round in a 4/4 pattern with an occasional flurry of atemporal insanity and strange irregular phrasing. Electronic and yet organic, historic even. They fed some internal, subconscious stream of thought that was intertwined with my circuits but wholly separate and distinct, feeding them with ecstasy, noise and smiles.

It felt like there was a pool of ferrofluid inside me and it was reacting to the frequencies, constructing some beautiful sculpture that only I could see and feel, sweet spikes of organometallic fluid pressing pressure points, cutting circuits here, connecting new ones there. I didn't ask her, but I was certain that Cilia was feeling it too. Jessica never connected us like we ought to have been. She never made things simple. She allowed us to operate each other's limbs and organs, but never connect mentally. A simple coder-transmitter-receiver-decoder system could have enabled Cilia and I to operate at double our efficiency. Our thoughts could run in tandem, a lightning storm between us. Lana would have been safe even now. Cilia could just think the correct course of action without me having to guess or ask.

"It is a list of parts to construct a drum."

"What?"

"The list. I looked it over. It lists the requisite parts to make a drum. And on the back is a diagram, with a small annotation stating that there will be a thousand made." Cilia was always one step ahead of me.

The old woman was asleep in our arms, cradling the cat as we cradled her. I wondered if it was a list made by whoever had created the drums that had begun to sound along with the original after the deluge.

"In the distance there are three large bonfires lit," Cilia said.

Excitation coursed through my wiring. We would soon be on our way to rescue Lana.

"It is beautiful," Cilia chimed. I never heard her chime before.

I was taken aback by the realization that I had never known, nor even considered what Cilia found beautiful before. I produced a simulated image of three fires burning in the distance at daybreak. Like miniature stars on the cusp of death, being beaten into obscurity by the rising sun. The contrast of the flames gaining an almost hallucinatory appeal as the day saturates the sky. The blue complimenting the orange flicker casually, like an old friend.

"I think I agree," I said to her.

"You wouldn't know beauty even if it came in discrete packets of data for you to analyze and organize."

I felt hurt. "You think you know beauty better than me?"

"Lana taught me. I know she didn't teach you anything but how to be a mule."

Lana and Cilia used to talk without me? I was more stung by this than by the flippant insult Cilia tried to slap me with. I was Lana's knight, her specially chosen partner who would be there as her rock and anvil, her sword and cushion. Cilia was the addition, the afterthought, the component there for aesthetic rather than functional purpose. She was quota filling, nothing more. Yet Lana had bonded with her all the same, perhaps even shared secrets with her that she hadn't with me. No, Cilia was lying. Cilia was rude and untrustworthy. Only, she wasn't. She had never lied to me before. She insulted me, and she pointed out my mistakes and shortcomings, but she never lied. Lana really must've been friends with Cilia as well as friends with me. I thought I saw everything of Lana, like she was some 2D drawing and I had torn the page out and hidden the pencil—there was nothing more to add. She was complete. But apparently I only had a sketch of her true character.

"Lana said that you wouldn't get it. You couldn't even see the glaring differences in all the

Jessicas over the years, so how could you see the subtleties of beauty?"

The Jessicas? I wasn't aware of multiple Jessicas.

"You never noticed that Jessica didn't get old like the other people."

I had a concept of Jessica, a data sheet, a series of discrete information, and my perception of Jessica corresponded to it every time I saw her. There was no reason to expect change in her appearance or essence. I didn't have that variable, her age. I wondered how old I was. I didn't understand why I had been made with incomplete knowledge of both Jessica and Lana. How could I have served them to the best of my ability without that knowledge?

"We are approaching the fires now. There are many people about. Most are dancing around the flames, smearing something over their flesh. The others appear to be in comas. It looks like a rave. You might want to think about running strafing defense protocol."

I hardly even noticed setting the protocol in motion; I was reeling from the information overload. I took the old lady and her cat from Cilia and holstered them, magnetic bars holding them in place against my thigh. She continued to snore deeply.

She didn't know anything at all about Lana or Jessica, or me or Cilia for that matter. Her world was probably made up of feeding and walking the cat. I felt good for a moment, before realizing that I didn't know anything about the cat. Even the old lady had secrets from me. I was in my own world, secluded from everything and everybody else. How long had I been alone?

"Cilia."

"Yes?"

"I was just checking you were still there."

"What? Of course I am, we're inseparable— much to my dismay."

We stopped running and Cilia patched me into her sensors again.

The amber from the fires soaked into the

clouds above like the whole world was engulfed by a soft sun. The people dancing around the fires had begun pulling trays off of them; it looked like maybe they were burning their hands doing it. I didn't understand why they weren't using gloves. But then I realized that it was just another hidden aspect of the world I would never know.

They carried the trays over to the comatose people and poured a fluid into their mouths. I wondered if maybe it was oil and whether the old lady would fit in here after all. Maybe she had been an oil addict for years, maybe that was what had sent her crazy for her cat.

I unholstered her and shook her awake. Her gums smacked as her eyes opened. "What do you want, you piece of shitty, rusty metal junk?"

I ignored her fervent anger. I figured it was just how she was when she woke up. Lana was the same, a crab with ultra-sharp and sensitive pincers first thing in the morning. "We have brought you to the shopping district. We expect you'll be safe from those people with the animals on their hands here."

"What's that? I can't hear you. There's a damned racket going on."

I forgot that she probably didn't have computer-controlled hearing so she couldn't amplify and diminish selected noises at will. The drums must have been deafening to her. I grabbed her wrist and she struggled briefly, but settled when she realized I was just going to tie the laserwire to her.

"We saved you from those psychos. They wanted to take your cat."

No response. I shook the wire and checked my port before reattaching it. Still no response. No wonder Lana was able to slip away undetected, the wire was faulty.

"Put me down! Can't you see you're hurting my cat?" The old lady kicked at my shin as I set her down. It didn't hurt. I wish I could have felt pain, felt like she did something to me. But I felt dead. I didn't know I could feel dead before then. But I understand death to be the state of unfeeling, uncaring, unmoving, unloving. That was me right then. A block of unconnected matter, floating through space-time without anything to anchor me to a present, to a place. Maybe that was why the comatose people were taking such copious amounts of oil; maybe they felt dead and wanted to die and the people feeding them were still alive and loved them and so fed them to kill them.

"There's a Turkish delight, a cat whose gums are slack." The old lady removed the laserwire and walked towards the bonfires.

That's when the first totem reared its ugly, naked-ass head.

Chapter 17

Jessica's daily demise has been a quick event, too quick really, and Mansell is feeling anxious. How could he expect to last an entire day without killing somebody? His family lies in tatters in the killing room and now he has nothing to do.

He stands upon his balcony, his pet by his side, and looks out across the ocean.

The water had been the harbinger of doom to most people. Those that survived cursed it, they cursed it and they hated it. The salty waves crushed their hopes of escape. But not Mansell's. To Mansell the water was a blessing, a chance to start over. The waves of oppression he had felt from every other living soul were now realized and directed back at the few remaining survivors. He had engineered it, of course. Not the apocalypse as such, but in the aftermath he had seized his opportunity to take control of The Installation. An evil genius knows no bounds to its creativity, which is something he has learned quickly. Cloning and artificial intelligence were child's play. He set his sights much higher. It will require some extreme effort on his part, but when it's done it will be something to marvel at.

He strokes one of the metallic heads of his cyborg idly whilst imagining the terror eating at his subordinates. Yes, his subordinates. They were so enamored with him they couldn't even see it, so blind and dependent they assumed their sight was perfect and they were free. He said 'take my hand friends, I will be your light and your way,' and they have clasped on like lost children as he leads them into the street where the merry cars will run them down like rabbits.

The electronic drums are nearing their peak. At least eight hundred are playing now. Lana is secure. It is nearly time for the end.

It really is quite beautiful, Mansell thinks, when you can click your fingers in time to some music and each click snuffs just that little bit more life out so that by the end of the song you're the only one left, just you and your snapping fingers, snapping, snap. And then you're gone too.

Chapter 18

The totem emerged over the horizon, like The Installation had morning glory. A giant phallic worm standing tall against the sky ready to penetrate into space. People scrambled up the sides like Moses up Mt. Sinai. I doubted there was a god atop those totems. The faces of the people already in the pile-up were in a mixture of confusion and ecstasy. It must be comforting to know that you're not the only one to have a crazy idea, that others will follow you no matter what.

"We have been followed," Cilia informed me. "Some of the animal-hands gang had tracker dogs stuffed onto their fists and they have hounded after us."

I spun around to see the gang turning up, their steeds mad from carrying their gross mass upon their backs. They hadn't even taken their fists out of the anuses of their pets and so sat at obtuse angles, awkwardly clinging onto their fur. I say their pets—I suspect that they may have stolen many of the animals. A fair few of the gang had scratch and bite marks worse than Cilia and I had.

"Where's the woman with the cat?" One of them challenged us, stepping right up to us.

"She has gone now," I told them. "You must leave the cat alone. It doesn't need your fist in its ass, it is perfectly happy on that leash."

"Besides," added Cilia from over my shoulder, "it doesn't even have teeth."

"Foolish cyborg, you think we want its teeth?" The guy sprung his hands up, on the ends were two Rottweilers, jaws gnashing like industrial grinders. "I've got fucking teeth." As if to emphasize his point he flashed his own, which were rotten and bleeding. "No, we want the cat because it'll be like getting a gummy blowjob every time we jerk off."

I snapped the man's neck in two places. His head hung like a ballsack from his shoulders. He crumpled to the floor and I squashed him like the bug he was, the small amount of brain putrefying in his skull squirted out like a sea cucumber's entrails. The dogs scrambled to their feet, regained a sense of where they were and ran away, his arms jutting out of their rears like two broom handles, dragging his limp dick body behind.

"Junk!"

"Cilia! I don't know what came over me!"

Every interaction I had seemed to end up with me killing the other person since those damned drums started acting up. I felt so calm about it too, like it was protocol. Protocol was to strike out and slaughter all others.

"No Junk, I don't give a shit about you killing people. The others are coming at us!"

She was right. They were approaching at just slower than breakneck speed.

I kicked at the nearest one, splitting their face and spilling their obviously inferior brain, before running away again.

"I don't understand Cilia, why do I keep hurting people?"

"I don't know Junk, it seems that you enjoy it."

A strange buzz of electricity cleared my mind, a vacuum filled by pleasant light. Maybe I lost Lana so I could find my true self. Maybe I was incapable of love after all and had always been looking for an outlet for my true potential. Maybe I lost Lana on purpose.

The drums were going crazy, elliptic beats so loud they dented my chest plate. The totem swerved across the sky as a small satellite appeared as it caught the rising sun's light. It raced across the sky as fast as a jet. Another totem emerged beside the first, wobbling as it learnt how to stand. The satellite came towards it, smashing the top clean off and smothering the new tip in flame. People fell to the ground like melted wax and the stench of bacon grilled too long quickly saturated the air, mixing in with the sweet, sickly aroma of the burning shops.

Another satellite rose from the horizon, a golden star ascending like a rocket. It arced and came down towards the first totem, which swung back the other way, narrowly avoiding being decapitated like its younger sibling. The satellite landed amongst the comatose people, setting a few alight. The others became animated by this turn of events and began to stand, their bodies were thick with concentrated oil, stored beneath their skin, so they looked like doughballs. The satellite rolled on past us and I was able to see it properly. It was one of the machine fetishists, curled up inside a tire.

"It just rolled over a few of our pursuers, but not enough to end the chase," Cilia warned me. "Keep running. I'm going to rest." She switched off, leaving me alone to brave the increasingly dangerous environment. I wasn't even sure which way to navigate myself. I had lost the instinct to find Lana. I felt like I wanted to be alone, so I was kind of grateful for the silence. But as I wasn't actually alone just yet I was also annoyed at Cilia for ditching me yet again in such a troublesome situation. I ran into the midst of the no-longer comatose people, the fires casting their shadows long and evil, so I felt at home.

I ran right through the dancing crowd and growing hulks of oil-saturated fat people and up a small brow. On the other side I saw the machine people gathered. There were more than before, a factory deconstructed and recomposed into a moving war machine. They launched more firebombs, screeching hail of light. They missed the totem as it dodged them, or flailed and tried to remain standing, and flew into the gang of animal abusers.

I made an executive decision to run to my left but became confused because I was looking behind me; I went right and ended up running off another cliff into Gimp Cove.

Chapter 19

"Your art is beautiful."

"Thanks Cilia, but you know you have to sound more genuine than that if you want me to believe you."

"Your art is beautiful."

"See, now that you're repeating the same thing I know it's not true. The tone you used was not genuine."

"Then why don't you teach me how to genuinely love art?"

Lana scratched her head, water colour paint staining her nails. Why was Cilia so interested in art all of a sudden? Had Lancelot been talking to her?

"Junk is a fool," Cilia said. "He is oblivious."

"Don't read my thoughts Cilia, that's rude."

Cilia purred.

"Besides, we're not talking about Junk now.

This is our time." Lana flicked her hair, a thousand years of art nor a thousand sunrises on Mars could compare to the majesty of each fine stroke of paint that dashed against her surroundings. "What does that make you feel Cilia?"

"I don't feel, I only think."

"Then what do you think?"

"I think it is a mess. I think you make a mess of things and people are ignorant. They confuse themselves by performing a complex series of redundant valuations and conclude that your art is something beautiful because they don't want to appear as ignorant as they are. I think that people do not like that things are as they appear and are scared if their own thoughts and feelings are real. They sublimate things they do not understand to avoid the difficulty in actually engaging them in any meaningful way."

Lana screwed her face up tight. "You're just jealous that I can do wonderful things with my hair and appreciate the playful nature of art."

"I don't know what jealousy is. I'm a cyborg,

Lana. I am designed to help you survive in this environment and to do that I am only required to compute things in terms of how well they benefit your survival. Your art is not objectively playful, nor is it particularly detailed. There is no emotion to it. Nothing invested in it. It happens for no reason other than you have paintbrush hair. People are afraid to accept this and they invent tableaux that contextualize the alien concepts in waxy falsehood."

"Then you'll never be able to appreciate art genuinely."

"Then I shall continue to appreciate it with honest disinterest." Cilia combed Lana's hair.

Chapter 20

The water hadn't always been so violent, so oppressive, possessed by some demon jealous of the land trying to swallow it down into its void, nullify its existence. But since the apocalypse the waves were unrelenting. Maybe the ocean was jealous that some life still clung to the land and merely wanted to grab it and drag it close to its heart, back to where it began. If so, it applied its love too roughly, smashing ships and drowning men before they'd even left the coast. Vessels burst under the pressure of waves. Insides voided like soft seaweed.

I switched the sonar on. The repetitive blip was almost lost amongst the sound of the tide crunching ship against rock and the hell drums above. A reef made of dead ships dimly emerged from the dark. A dead body. Gargantuan and full and paradoxically so empty. Glistening currents reflected whispers like ephemeral curtains cast out to sea.

Dead eye sockets sunken and flooded stared at me as I descended into the depths of Gimp Cove, their hollowness echoing back at me. Even something as supposedly benign as the sea can take a man's light, his sight, his life. What kind of horror am I capable of?

My feet touched the bottom. A wooden ship destined for greatness, chewed by the jaws of the sea, rested on its side, algae digesting it. The soft rotten planks of the hull disintegrated as I landed on them and I fell further down into the belly of the corpse. The bony arms of fragmented sailors lost to their home, their family, their friends, engulfed me in an embrace like I was a sorely missed child come home. Distant snare shots reverberated like party poppers in a far away room while a bass the size of the titanic sounded like an army stomping on my head. Salt water corroded my insides, making my sensor contort through all the different settings. I had plunged into a deep sea disco.

In amongst the floating corpses of desperate men, flooded by more than just the desire to escape the confines of the Installation, were storage containers marked by an official looking seal. I flipped the lid of the nearest one, the lock degraded over the decade or so it had been lying idle, and felt around inside. The soothing touch of a cold metal cylinder greeted my palms. Another one, partially attacked by algae but still alluring in the smooth manner in which it fanned out into an exhaust. I felt back the other way, fingers tracing the faint outline of a chest compartment, the bumpy exterior of a radiator, the subtle décor of a starter motor, the thick rubbery cables connecting it to the battery encased in its own private compartment. I hoped they made these things waterproof as standard. I slung the jet pack over a shoulder, careful not to damage sleeping Cilia's head, and sat to figure out a way to escape the watery confines of this lonely hearts disco.

Chapter 21

The sunset paled behind a thin layer of mucus cloud lining the horizon. Lana's soft singing was reminiscent of lost wildlife she had never heard, autumnal breezes playing in the forest. I turned my head because the wilderness of the sea was depressing, and Lana's voice suddenly sounded like distorted cars in a city centre all slowly crunching into each other and sounding their horns as they flattened into non-dimension juxtaposed onto a million computers overheating and arguing like siblings on a boat lost at sea. She still looked like the girl I always cherished, but her voice dragged across the ground, mud slowing it, killing it.

She turned and looked at me, wild puzzlement like two stars in her pupils. "What's wrong, Lancelot?"

"Nothing's wrong Lana. I just thought you

sounded unique and beautiful."

Her face formed in a way I hadn't ever seen before she turned away from me. "You're silly, Junk. Of course I'm unique. There's only one of me!"

Chapter 22

Morning heralds across the water's surface, white light riding the waves into the rocks where it breaks apart like the ships, like the hearts of the survivors as they saw their hopes for redemption disintegrate into useless wood and junk. We burst from the ocean like a wet phoenix, a satellite relaunched into orbit, propelled by history itself. The intake pipes of the jet pack sound like a sherbet string quartet on speed, the pounding drums, their sickening percussion accompaniment, the interstellar blast of compressed fuel and air a brass bass section underpinning the entire suite. We soar as the birds we'll never know again.

The machine people are slaughtering the do-gooders who were stupid enough to continue to try to feed their comatose friends. Bones, hair and flesh sizzle on the open fire as they are smashed aside by pneumatic limbs. The animal-fisted are fighting back; their teeth and claws scratch metal and flesh, but to no avail. The animals' heads are destroyed and the hosts torn to pieces by engineered death limbs. There are more towers made of people, seven all together. Two become infernos as suicide machine bombers crash into their sides. They crumble into flame, spreading like goo across the land. I hear the dying screams of the flesh even over the symphony played by the jet pack. Even over the dread drums, numbering in their hundreds.

Chapter 23

A thousand years of art history entombs us, compresses our skulls together, trying to impress upon us the importance of their role in the social and economical advances humanity has made over the centuries. In the dark, all art is junk. A subversive gravity holding me down. Useless weight preventing me from reaching Lana. I lash out at the canvasses become coffins, tearing them to shreds. It's not enough though. I become a tornado, twisting my way through the subterranean art world, uprooting sculptures and deconstructing them, blurring pieces together into hybrid art that I entertain is original for a moment before destroying it, too. I peel layers away from the world and chew them up and digest them so that they came become the literal shit they figuratively are. Centuries collapse into nothing as I engulf their history. Higher up I see future art begin to fall, its support eaten away. I chew my way through modern art, bland, tasteless and sharp. Post-modern art is a thick wall of gunk. I try to eat it but I become assimilated into it. Price tags pass across my chest, a barcode erupts on my skin before becoming a digital mosaic somewhere in my intestine. Fingertips touch my screen, they slide me around a dimension inside myself, grease smears across my face.

"Ugly."

"Regurgitated crap."

"Artistically handicapped."

Judgments passed and branded, I am lost into a pit of user-rated garbage. No price tag. No value. I am obsolete data. I am Junk.

Chapter 24

The wall of sludge spits us out onto a concrete floor coated with a layer of oil. I know it's coated in oil because we slide across it. We slide across it into a drum. And not just any drum. One of the dread drums. An army of drums resound in atemporal dissonance. The sheer intensity is beating us senseless. Cilia's sensor spasms, my vision flicks through six million colours, x-ray and ultraviolet. It finally settles, everything tinted teal and orange.

The beaters are made of the decapitated heads of children. They smash face-first into the drum skin, secreting a fluid on every beat. As I reach out and catch some of the expelled fluid I'm shocked and appalled by the discovery that it's oil. The miracle escape drug that fuels people's dreams is the brain juice of their dead future. If I had a stomach it would be on the floor, contents sprawled like an organic replica of Cilia and I.

I scream, "Cilia!" but she doesn't respond. I don't know how she is managing to sleep through this nightmare onslaught. I unsteadily rise to my feet, take a step, and slip on my ass. I try again, this time grabbing onto the nearest beater. The skull is soft like cheese and squeezes through my fingers like paste. The mechanism it's attached to is really strong too, and I'm whipped around as it strikes the drum. I go right through the skin and into the body of the drum.

The blood of a countless number of children sloshes out like a tsunami at dawn as the skin tears. I stand up inside the drum and scream. I scream until my voice modulator breaks and I'm frying circuitry. It's fine that my voice is cracked and can only come out as hobbled specks of light, like microscopic stars, because I know there's nothing more to say. I begin to walk away from the drum. Blood the colour of rust dries on my skin and cracks as I wade through the ocean of blood, though it looks more like orange juice, brain matter like pulp. I take in the area. A large atrium. The drums are still blasting us with concentrated harmonic waves, curling the sheet metal plating on my shoulders, bending it into wavy artforms. The chamber must be designed to project the acoustics perfectly. Amplify the destructive wave fronts. I see a large valve ahead; it opens and closes regularly, sucking the sound out of the hall. That must be the only reason we haven't been completely demolished by the sound waves yet.

I crawl across the room and the valve inhales us into a pipe as drum strikes ricochet around us.

Chapter 25

A happy coincidence led Mansell to discover oil. His cyborg was busy pasting the head of his ugliest child into the wall when the fluid oozed out of their head like tears. So thick it was like sap. Unsure as to what exactly it was Mansell ordered his cyborg to take him to his laboratory immediately.

He had performed numerous tests on his other children and came away with conclusive results. The complete annihilation of their consciousness and hope produced a rich solute high in concentrate of potential and dreams, the likes of which he had never seen before. Under a microscope it was possible to see their futures coalesce before unfurling and disintegrating, endless myriad forms of life; stockbrokers, politicians, artists, mechanics, doctors and more careers that didn't even exist yet. Innumerable tubes of light twisted and found each other like lovers' limbs, penetrated and sliced each other. Newborn lives burst from their insides and gave birth themselves. A beautiful fractal display of microcosmic evolution.

It was disgusting.

Seeing so much life that would never look up to him, would more than likely belittle and deride him for his insignificance, his evil. The evil that same life created no less!

***

"This will hurt a lot, but it's more than you deserve," he said to his unwilling subject as he soaked some of the oil up into a syringe. He stepped in front of the child strapped in place on the easel. A beautiful girl, his favorite out of all he had produced in fact. "You know, of all the runts, you're my favorite." Her hair was thick like paintbrush bristles, a meadow of wildflowers painted on her scalp. He suspected his artistic streak had probably been more strongly enunciated in her than any of the others. But it was too little, too late. Life had been a bitch and now he was going to be a bitch back.

He rubbed her forearm, encouraging the blue pigment veins to show themselves and they popped up across her paper-white skin like flowers in the winter. The needle secreted a small globule of fluid, the color and consistency of pre-cum as he placed it against her skin.

"Daddy," her little voice pleaded. "You're a cock!" He heard her mind scream.

"No Lana, not now."

He swore the fluid brimmed with excitement as he was about to push down on the syringe, but it may have just been his own nerves causing him to shake. Seemingly out of nowhere a robotic hand jerked his arm holding the needle aside. Mansell drew himself back in fear, expecting his life to blink out any moment. When the head-crushing pressure didn't come he uncovered his head, to discover the child gone and in her place, Jessica, holding the needle against her neck like a suicidal person with a gun.

His penis squirmed around in his briefs, crusty blood vessels filling with blood for the first time in a decade or more. He grabbed at it, yanking it free of his pants. It hung like a derelict sewerage outlet, a wire shrubbery of pubic hair growing from it like a morbid mold. The end was chapped, leper-like. The skin had long since drained of vitality. Still, it stood on its own, which gave Mansell a surge of confidence, confidence he used to approach Jessica and kiss her on the lips.

"I always loved you, Jessica," he said as they stared into each other's eyes.

"I know, Mansell. I know."

He plunged the needle into her neck, injecting her with the potent drug, the years of humanity lost to his violent need for retribution.

Her eyes formed galaxies, her vagina swelled until it burst, her clitoris became so swollen it hit the ground. Nipples jabbed him in the ribs and didn't stop there, pressing into his lungs, diffusing into his blood stream, coursing through his arteries, into his balls. He felt her steal his semen, his sperm, his potential, but he didn't mind; Jessica's thoughts stroked him in a way he never thought possible. Life smiled on Mansell as he collapsed like a broken chair. His penis churned out a puff of smoke and deflated.

"That was sensational!" Jessica said. He watched as she placed his sperm into a tube and bent over him. "Thanks for that, jerk off." She thought. "Thanks for that, Mansell," she said and walked away.

The orgasm had stolen his voice. It was okay though; he knew there was nothing more to say. He felt the bud of a nipple tucked neatly in his lung, a bullet with Jessica's DNA in it.

Chapter 26

"What happened to your parents, Lancelot?" Lana stops painting and looks up at me.

"I don't have any parents, Lana."

"Of course you do, silly. Even a complete robot has parents, and you aren't even completely robotic."

"I don't know then. Perhaps you should ask Cilia."

Lana strokes me with a blue brush; the sky never looks as beautiful as that strip of paint on my chest.

"I want to know about your parents, not hers."

"Jessica made both me and Cilia together. Maybe she is our mother?"

"Then we'd be brother and sister. I've always felt like you're my big brother, Lancelot."

I smile and paint Lana's nose orange like the

sun she is.

Chapter 27

I kick a large speaker cover out from in front of us and jump to the ground some ten feet below. The wailing noise of the drums follows us out like an army of ghosts. We're in an area of the Installation I don't recognize, collages of words jumbled together in nonsensical ways like a Burroughs novel disorientating me to no end. I switch my English comprehension circuit off.

Climb exec. Run.

Climbing.

Climb exec. Complete.

Scan exec. Run.

Scanning.

Scan exec. Complete.

Object. Define. Fix. 35°.

Auxiliary Motile function exec. Run.

Running. Object clarify.

Desist motile function in 5, 4, 3, 2, 1, 0.

Desist Complete.

Auxiliary Motile function exec. Complete.

Object fix. 0.001°. Resolution. Scan for written language.

Complete.

No language detected.

Language selection protocol exec. Run.

Language select: English. Running.

Language selection protocol exec. Complete.

System check exec. Run.

System check exec. Complete.

Voice emulator destroyed. Searching for alternative.

Searching.

Search complete. Alternative found. Switching system to alternative.

Reboot to install. Reboot exec. Run.

Reboot in 3, 2, 1, 0.

[.][..][...][x][0][01][1][BOOT]

Boot exec. Run.

Boot exec. Complete.

"Incoming projectile. Run!" Hearing Cilia's voice is so soothing and reassuring that I almost fail to hear her screeching. Luckily she takes the initiative and engages her power jump thrust protocol, sending us through the wall in front of us and into a living area.

A flaming ball of metal screams and follows us through the hole we made and I roll to the side just as it comes hurtling past. It crashes into the wall on the far side, setting fire to the world around it.

"Remove us from the vicinity, Junk," Cilia orders me, her voice edged with crackling disharmonious electricity like diamonds made of anger. I comply by running over the flaming wreck and through the wall. We enter a kitchen.

A woman is deftly slicing vegetables on a side with her back to us, chopping one up with nimble blade work before grabbing another from a stack beside her. She seems to be oblivious to our intrusion and I think it best if we keep it that way. We side-step out of the door I notice to my left.

The hallway is decorated with elaborate

artwork—canvasses made of stretched skin. A surreal art installation lit by a swinging sodium bulb. There are doors between the artwork hanging like a series of family portraits but I don't want to go through any of them. I see a glass window at the far end, gently smudged by the rain outside, and head straight for it. I'll find Lana again.

The door to our left swings open and a giant metal limb engulfs us.

Chapter 28

Jessica stands over her dead body. It lays in parts, torso, head and legs. The machine people have taken her artificial hips to fix their machine gun emplacements, giving them full articulation.

The world is littered with dead Jessicas. They are almost as numerous as the number of dead children Mansell has been raising. Her gums clack together as the rain softens her lips, softens her skin. The cat tugs on the lead. In the distance a totem collapses.

"There's a Turkish delight, a cat whose gums are slack!" She yanks the cat towards her and it acquiesces and rubs its face on her leg. The small phial on its collar jingles as it nushes against her old, worn-away shin, skin so thin it's become translucent, like the faded pages of an old book. She walks on, ignoring the gun fire and bombs and cat screeches and death drums all working together to create a warzone around her. She has only one destination in mind. Only one place she needs to be.

Chapter 29

The mechanical arm pulls us into a laboratory. It deposits us into a vat and shuts a lid above us. It's completely dark inside.

"Cilia?"

"Fuck off, Junk. I'm sleeping."

"Cilia, we're in trouble, I think."

"You're in trouble. You're crushing my head."

I apologize and scramble to the side. "We're in a vat, Cilia. I don't know how to get out."

"Why not Houdini gut punch your way out?"

Good old Cilia, always there when the moment is right. Sure, she can be snappy when she's tired, but she's so logical it hurts.

"Houdini gut-punch!" I cry as I slam my fist into the side of the vat. It dents a little, but overall the effect is not as grand as I had hoped.

"It didn't work."

"Try again then, you idiot!"

Good old Cilia, always sharp-witted and quick as a bolt to come up with logical solutions to problems.

"HOUDINI GUT PUNCH!" My fist pops through the vat like a metal spike. I stretch the opening wide like a vagina birthing a child. As I crown I see the robotic arm that put us here, and the monstrous machine it's attached to. I almost regret getting out.

The thing is huge and has two dinosaur heads. Its eyes are as red and evil as the devil's asscheeks. Although it makes no move, I am sure it has its sights set on us. As if to confirm that's the case, it fires lasers from all four of its eyes, disintegrating the vat around us. We fall as a lump of potential coal to the ground.

"Cilia?" Mechanical breathing and a hum like a lullaby. The bitch is asleep! I'm alone again. I stare at the creature through Cilia's scope.

"Ah, Lancelot, Cilia, I'm thrilled you've

arrived!"

I crackle inside. Somebody has stolen my voice. I don't mean just that my module is destroyed, I mean that I am hearing myself talking outside of my body and the words aren't originating in my mind.

"What on earth happened to your face, Lancelot? You look like you've been through a war! I'll fix that up before long, don't worry."

Maybe I died, maybe I didn't realize it but the laser-eyed cyborg across the room has already murdered me and I'm having an out-of-body experience. My mind thinks I'm still in my body but actually I'm way outside of it. It's relaxing to know I don't have any responsibilities anymore, that I'm free to move as I wish. I failed Lana, but at least I died trying to correct that mistake. If this is the afterlife, well, it's not quite as wonderful as religious texts make out, but I do have a sense of completion, like, what's done is done.

The twin-headed dinosaur cyborg picks us up like a puppy, like we are its puppy. I've never felt so cared for, so helpless. This must be how Lana felt in my arms, or maybe I'm romanticizing. Either way, I don't feel like I'm in danger, in fact, I feel loved. We are put down onto a tabletop and the voice says we'll feel a little sleepy and then everything will be okay, and I trust it because it's my voice telling me that.

Chapter 30

My sensor wakes up and the world feels fresh. Trident light tickles my circuitry. The green is the green of newborn leaves, the red the beautiful sunrise, the blue a crisp sky bulb delirious and full of the joy of spring. My joints slide around without a complaint, my circuits shoot current as fast as lightning. I sit up. A female torso sans legs is hanging opposite me. Multicolored wires hang from the holes at the bottom of her thighs where her femurs should be. They look like veins and arteries and lymphs and nerves.

"You know why I don't mind cyborgs like you, Lancelot?"

I tell myself I'm alive, even though I hear my voice talking to me from somewhere far away. I'm alive and I'm not crazy. Somebody just stole my voice.

"How did you get my voice?" I say,

surprised to notice that now my voice comes out of me.

"What?" I ask myself from outside myself.

I look around and see a man standing beside the dinosaur cyborg. He tenderly strokes its head.

"How did you get my voice?"

"Let me tell you now, I am just as surprised to hear you with my voice as you are to me with yours, Lancelot," He says. He doesn't sound surprised.

"Who are you?" I ask, straining my neck to try and get a good look at him. My head feels strangely light, like it would flop forward if I didn't constantly guard against it.

"My name is Mansell Rivers. I trust you know the name, Jessica would have told you."

"Mansell Rivers." My fist cracks diamond dimensions into dust. "We are to kick you until you die."

"We?"

"Cilia and I."

"Ah, Cilia, dear sweet Cilia. You mean that

thing hanging like a fish at a market?"

I look at the torso again. Of course I didn't recognize her; I've never seen Cilia's face before. She is truly beautiful. Her face a mask of butterfly make-up, probably painted on by Lana. She looks strangely reminiscent of Lana, but I figure that's due to my limited experience with women rather than any objective similarity.

I turn back to Mansell. "What have you done with Lana?" I feel like I snarl aggressively, but I'm also terrified so it probably comes off as a terrier type of bark.

"Last I heard she was in one of the totems. I will be dealing with her presently. You know, it was so difficult to get her to take the oil. Must have memories of our time together when she was still very young. But that is all beside the point. Do you know why I don't mind cyborgs, Lancelot?"

"No."

Mansell walks up close to me. Sweat clings to his brow like a disease. His lab coat is dirty, dirty like the world is dirty. "Because you aren't telepathic." He smiles, like what he says means something. But I'm not telepathic, so I don't know what he's thinking.

I have no idea why that would mean he doesn't mind us. I mean me. Why he doesn't mind me. I've always wanted to be telepathic. I can't recall why. I mean, it must've been for pragmatic reasons, but now I don't know what those reasons were. I guess they didn't matter in the long run.

I must've been silent for too long because Mansell makes a noise like he's getting impatient. Did he ask me something else? Maybe he was just testing to be sure I wasn't telepathic. What kind of evil things was he thinking about me just then?

"It makes me sad to think that Jessica wasted my potential on a thing like you when she could have crafted something like my tyrannosaur over here. You share the same DNA, you know."

The tyrannosaur snorts and laughs mockingly.

"It's true. You are essentially alternative versions of each other, of me and Jessica. My version is course, far superior to Jessica's—to you, that is."

"But how?"

"Replicating DNA was one of the things your mother, Jessica, was good at. It wasn't long before I stole the concept and used it to my own nefarious ends."

Suddenly Mansell looks like he's a weak ghost. Like his soul is one last jab away from disintegrating. Like his entire life is built on a self-eroding principle and he's nearly out of spirit.

"And now, if you don't mind. I am going to destroy the remaining life on the planet."

Mansell walks away, followed by his pet. By us. Cilia and I. Jessica and Mansell. By him. By me.

Chapter 31

Cilia is asleep. She looks just like Lana, only her legs are missing and she doesn't have paintbrush hair. Lancelot is crying to himself. Poor Lancelot. Just like his father. It must be hard to come to terms with finding out you are the enemy you always fought to avoid.

Jessica strokes the cat. It gums her wrist, but doesn't bite too hard.

She says, "Lancelot. You shouldn't cry. You're a knight."

Lancelot looks at her through a blurred sensor. "Lana?"

"No silly, it's me, Jessica."

"But you died."

"So many times, I know. But I'm here now, and I need you to rescue Lana. She's the key. Mansell must not get her."

Lancelot shakes his head. "No, I am Mansell, I will only end up hurting her myself."

"No Lancelot, you are your own person. You are what Mansell could have been if he had allowed himself to grow as a person instead of sealing himself away from the world."

"But Jessica, the children, it was horrific." Lancelot finally looks at her again.

"That was not your fault. And if you really want to stop that from happening, you must rescue Lana." Jessica hugs him tightly. Her flesh is cold, ancient. The cat mews beside her. She stops hugging him and unhooks the cat's collar. "Here, take this," she says as she passes him a phial. "It contains oil. But not that kind of oil. This oil comes from the heart. My heart. Give it to Lana. She'll know what to do."

Jessica fades into tracing paper translucency, and then into nothing at all. The cat snuggles into Lancelot's chest and goes to sleep.

Chapter 32

I resuscitate Cilia. She hangs like a marionette with no operator, all sunken and sorrowful.

"I'll find you some legs."

She doesn't complain as I fix tank tracks to her thighs. "It was the best I could do," I say apologetically.

Cilia nods. "Thanks, Lancelot."

I shake my head. "I am Junk."

"You are a knight."

"And you are my steed." I climb aboard Cilia. The world is pumping mad drum schisms and blaring flaming guns and bombs as we roll out like a fucking war machine on steroids.

Chapter 33

Geyser-pumping madness atmosphere. An erotic sewer angel heaven catastrophe. Teeth clicking like bullet cases, starlight falling to the floor. Hercules' balls aflame and aloft. Totems made of faces, made of singing collapse. Fat guises, distort, blend, disturb. All oil-slick sugar-skin. Metal orgy feast on oil on kingdoms on art installations gone wrong. The world is flickered with electron paint, buzzing honey city lights lost to perdition a night long winter soiled by drums transforming dreams to wakeful vengeful child song.

And all the while, she bangs along, and, strangely alone, calling in Morse code for sleeper cell amnesia to melt the ruse to silence the drums to drown the world to destroy all art, she asks of Gaia, redemption.

Chapter 34

Cilia's tank tracks make short work of crossing the pulped landscape. The fire has burnt most of the crust away, revealing eroded signs and symbols, blackness beneath. They all burn to charcoal black in the end.

The Installation is a mess. Is it still art when the audience is dead?

Only one totem remains, far taller and grander than any before it. The top of the totem spreads like angel wings, the sun behind it like heaven's light welcoming it to the kingdom above. No doubt brought about by the drug they've all been ritually injecting. It's a new way of living, built on hollowness and ruptured organs. I super-zoom in on the totem and see their faces, mouths plastic melted scars, eyes tubes bending the world to suit their view. Machine people casting off their armor, frail limbs droop and sway. Animal-fisting grotesques scratched and bitten, fighting their own weapons.

Even the comatose, their feeders and the shops, all stacked like ornaments, a middle finger stuck up at God.

The totem is shrinking by the second. Mansell and his cyborg are hacking at the base. A geyser of blood erupts from the totem with every swing of its machete arms.

"Cilia, charge!" I yell atop my steed, and she complies. We're only three hundred feet from it now.

Mansell spies us coming and climbs on his own cyborg. He fires twin lasers at us and Cilia darts like a nimble lizard to avoid them. Where they land the world becomes a void. The cyborg changes tactic as it realizes it won't be able to hit agile Cilia, and so fires a wide laser beam about fifty feet ahead of us, cutting The Installation in two. The world separates, us on one side, them on the other, Lana on the other. To make it worse, the cyborg transforms into a gorilla and begins ascending the totem like a micro King Kong up an organic Empire State Building. Chunks of people fall away like debris as it uses them for leverage.

"Junk, you must save Lana," Cilia says. Her voice sounds like Jessica.

"I know, Cilia, but how?"

Cilia doesn't answer. She revs her engine so hard it sounds magnificent, and accelerates towards the gaping wound in the ground ahead.

"I love you, Junk," she says as we near the edge.

"I love you too, Cilia," I reply. I don't know what she's doing. She doesn't have the power jump thrust protocol anymore.

Then it hits me as Cilia hits the brakes. I am thrown forward like a rocket, heading straight at the totem. I look backwards to see Cilia topple over the cliff edge into the void. The most illogical thing I have ever seen her do.

Chapter 35

"You really are beautiful, Lana."

"Aren't all people, Lancelot?"

Maybe. Maybe not. People are shades and they are shadows and they take the shape of the world around them. But not Lana. Lana is special. She is the object casting the light.

"Not all people, Lana."

Chapter 36

I smash into the totem, collapsing a comatose person's side. Their fat flesh stops me deader than a solid wall ever could. I immediately begin to climb as fast as I can, gripping metal, skin, animal, clothes, whatever. I spy Mansell on the back of the monkey cyborg; he's close to the top. To Lana.

I see her, at the peak, the source of the light. Brighter than the sun. Mansell is within a few seconds of reaching her when she jumps. She falls past him, though her descent seems so slow he could reach out and grab her easily. I don't know what else to do so I throw the phial out towards her.

She grabs it out of the air, smiles, and falls into the bowels of The Installation. I look up and see Mansell descending on the back of his cyborg. I leap out as they pass, sending us flying towards the abyss.

Chapter 37

The ground absorbs our hearts and makes us think of gentler times. I mean, the ground absorbs my heart and makes me think of a gentler time. Cilia is gone. I pick myself up and am immediately tossed aside by a viciously strong arm.

"You had to come and fucking ruin everything didn't you, Junk."

I look at the source of the voice. Mansell stands next to the behemoth cyborg he has constructed.

"You made me think I was evil. I thought maybe I enjoyed killing people, maybe I lost Lana on purpose. But now I know that's just the weak part of me, the shit I got from you. I am here to stop *you* from ruining everything, Mansell." I spit blood and diodes onto the ground. "The Installation has my heart, there's nothing you can do."

"I can crush your soul and crumple your

body just enough that you don't die, but live on in excruciating discomfort."

Just like him.

"Can you, or do you need your pet dinosaur there to do it for you?"

A sharp kick to my ribs dissuades gravity for a moment as I soar into the air. Feeling more confident, gravity tugs me back to Earth aggressively.

"Don't speak ill of my perfect creation. My greatest artwork. That's what got the world in trouble in the first place." Mansell places a boot on my head. "I fucking hate cyborgs. And I fucking hate art." He attempts to squish my head. I am sure of it. The veins on his forehead pop out like worms in the rain. My head remains firmly in its normal state.

"You hate cyborgs?"

"I meant other cyborgs, Jessica, Jesus. I don't hate you, I love you," Mansell says seemingly apropos of nothing.

"See, you can't hurt me, Mansell."

"Fuck off, Junk." He puts even more force into trying to crush my skull but it's useless, the man's just weak.

The dinosaur seems to be conversing with itself. I think it might be telepathic.

"If you love me then why do you kill me every day?"

"For fuck sake, Jessica! Really, we're gonna do this now? I have to kill you because you and all the other cocksuckers out there belittle me. I will stop killing you once I have killed Lana."

"How do you know?"

"I just do. It's a fucking premonition. I kill Lana, I get closure."

"But how do we know you won't just keep killing us?"

Mansell is really acting strange. He is kneeling on my head now, using his forearms to squeeze my head like a spot. The metal is too strong for him, though. I decide enough is enough and fling him off me like the mite he is.

"Mansell Rivers, I am to kick you to death,"

I say, and feel good about it, like I'm killing the demon inside me.

"Jessica, stop him!"

The dinosaur moves quickly, gets between me and Mansell.

"You don't understand. Mansell is a bad man," I tell it. "He must die. I must kill him."

"He isn't a bad man. He's just very confused."

"Fuck you, Jessica!" Mansell screams and hammers his fists on her back.

"He's responsible for the death of everything that is good. He's a fucking child murderer!"

"No. I murdered those children, Lancelot. I could have said no. But I did it. I am as guilty as he is. If you want to kill him for being a child murderer, you have to kill me too."

Shit. I plan a variety of different attacks, but they all end with me being lasered in the face and having my brain melted.

"I don't want to have to kick your ass, Jessica. Stand aside." I try to be macho, but I know

I come across as a little machine that has bitten off more than it can process.

"Negative." Her eyes twinkle and a moment later, a laser blast scorches my arm to cinders. I dive, but the damage is done. She's too quick. I roll over and get kicked in the face, hard. My jaw slides across the floor away from me. I roll again, this time the opposite way and manage to scramble to my feet as Jessica comes flying at me, rockets propelling her in a flying dragon kick. She crunches into my chest, crumpling my shield and pressuring my battery. I feel acid bubble through my flesh, eating me away. We go flying backwards for another twenty feet before we land on the ground, Jessica's boot still planted in my chest.

"We'll tell Lana you said goodbye."

This is my only chance, I use my good arm to grab onto one of the heads and twist that fucker like it's a nipple and I'm a bully. It pops off and I use it to bash the other head as hard as I can. Jessica screams like a bitch and falls to the floor. I get up, bloody circuits and frying flesh stinking through my nostrils, and stuff the head on my shoulders, where Cilia ought to be. The eyes light up ruby red and laser bolts fire manically in all directions; it must still be delirious from the cranial collision I put on it. I jump onto my belly as Jessica stands back up and leaps at me. A laser shoots straight at her face, bursting it like a *piñata full of electronic sweets. Her cyborg body drops and splats like an egg.*

I grab the dinosaur head on my back and rip it off. It dies in my hands. After taking a moment to thank my lucky stars, I stand up.

Mansell is cowering on the ground, near the void.

He begs me not to kill him. He tells me he understands he was wrong. The sound of the drums mashing his children's faces drown out his words.

I was going to kick him until he died. But I can think of something more fitting. I drop him down the abyss, his screams echoing like a thousand children being slain.

Chapter 38

I can feel my insides turning black as I call to Lana; it's no use because I don't have the wireless module. Electricity leaks from my pours and my processor scrambles instructions like they're translated through three hundred languages. Ruptured joints stretch and crack and metal dissolves in weak acid.

My flesh unravels like millions of cables or worms or snakes or tubes of hollow light and my sensors melt. Lana cries, sitting on my shoulder.

"Daddy, I don't want to paint anymore. Art makes me sad. It's what keeps us in this sad world."

I grill my processor just to whir and purr at her, a Turkish cat with no gums.

Cilia erupts from the ground. Tank-like and charming.

Lana says, "Jessica, Mother, I want to leave this place," and walks towards Cilia.

I smile electronically. Pillars of people collapse like Jenga stacks whose foundations have been pulled apart. Cilia transforms into a boat and slowly glides out on the water. Lana pours the oil from the phial over her head. Paint falls from her hair, painting a pathway only she can walk along. The tears on her cheeks glint and fall and become mere drops in the ocean.

ABOUT THE AUTHOR

R. A. Harris writes with fury from his home in England. Some of his work finds its way into the hands of legitimate publishers. The rest is published at his blog: www.leakylibido.wordpress.com

BIZARRO PULP PRESS

 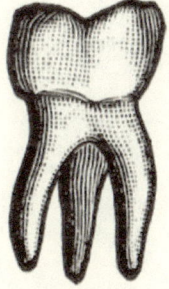

WWW.BIZARROPULPPRESS.COM